I0456995

# 3
## SHORT TALES OF
# RED

Three Short Tales of Red
*Copyright © 2014 by K.M. Tremills, Kathryn Cottam and Roberta Cottam*

*Cover illustration © 2014 by Roberta Cottam*

*Book design by Laura Wrubleski*

Print Edition: September 2014
ISBN: 978-0-9921020-9-8

Ebook Edition: October 2014
ISBN: 978-0-9921020-8-1

Published: 2014

Published by: Fox Tale Press

www.thefoxtalepress.com

*Red Riding Hood.*
Such a familiar story…
or is it?

# THE
# RED ONE

K.M. TREMILLS

WE'D BEEN WATCHING THE CHILD for a long time. She had a tendency to wander into the woods, like an innocent babe that did not understand the darkness that awaited her. The world is not a simple place. Much as she might wish it so.

Though the woods, by far, are a kinder place than the human world. When I speak of danger lurking amongst the trees, I do not speak of animals, unless they have turned rabid. No. Any threat in the dark spaces of the woods comes in the form of man.

As with most things, humans have the truth backwards. The moment they donned clothing, they separated from us. The day they built towns, humans believed they were superior. And the year they put walls around their towns, they decided we were the source of all darkness.

Humans could build all the stone structures in the world. They could never deny that they spawned from beast. They were born of the woods. The more fervently they denied that they belonged to the realm of blood, bone, and fur, the more their deviant ones claimed leadership that led them further astray.

They courted death with their tribal disagreements, yet somehow, humans refused to see they held fast to the ways of the pack. They dressed up their battles in vibrant colours and elegant music, but war was war. Whether it was fought with metal sticks or claws and fangs. They were as feral as the day they left the forest.

The humans had forgotten, but we did not. We knew their heritage. Besides, the wildness was not an element to be feared. No. We all bear the mark of the wild. A howl that frees the heart and sings to the soul of the earth. Why would they deny such a power? Such a beautiful, rhythmic way of living? I could not understand.

And the more they denied the truth, the stronger the call to the shadows.

They lit their streets with electric bulbs, chasing away shadows as though they did not belong. As though humans could decide that they were above all other creatures. But just as surely as the sun belongs to the day and the moon belongs to the night, we carry both. We must acknowledge both.

Otherwise, the creatures of the dark corners get restless and demand their due. Like any being told he does not exist. The act of denial is infuriating. They lash out. Or growl in a corner, feeding on anger and resentment, until the right moment appears for revenge. No one likes being trapped in a box and denied that she exists. Least of all the shadows.

And that is when the trouble began.

As I said earlier, we had been watching the child for many a year. She would enter the woods on the hard days. When the humans in her world had been particularly cruel. I could feel the pain in her heart. The confusion in her mind. And so she sought solace with the old ones. The tall ones. The ones who always listened.

For no one had the patience of the trees. Especially cedars. They had more tolerance than any other creature of the earth. They had witnessed more acts of love, hate, betrayal, and outrage than any other being. And still they stand, quiet and proud.

Believing in their gentle ways. Never changing.

When the Red One came dancing into the woods, swinging on their trunks, each cedar longed for her touch. For as much darkness as this girl of sixteen years had witnessed, she was one of the purest heart.

As her foot crossed into the sacred woods, all the trees whispered a prayer of protection. They shielded her with love. She must have felt their attentiveness because, when she walked among them, she shed the caution and care that burdened her soul. And became, once again, her true self. Guileless, kind, and filled with joy.

Each touch of her hand sent shivers up the spines of the cedars. Their bark would tremble as her surge of adoration touched their souls. They had not felt such reverence since the days they were worshipped as gods. Long ago, when humans still honoured the allegiance they had sworn to the old ones in the ancient gardens.

But those days were long gone. As each year passed, the humans forgot a little more. And a little more. Until they forgot altogether and swung their axes with abandon. Sending ancient elders to the ground without even a whisper of thanks. Tearing apart generations of families and casting aside millennia of mutual care.

So when the girl with the red locks came into the woods, the cedars held their breath. Her essence reverberated with the veneration of days gone by. The trees were taken off guard. Who was this child that felt like the people of the garden? The ones who acted like brethren to the creatures of fur, feather, and bark?

The cedars began to whisper among themselves. Was she a sign? Would this girl being back the hope of yesteryear? Or was she simply a lost child seeking the comfort of a temporary hideaway, oblivious to the difference she made to the ancient hearts of trees?

I peered around the curve of one of the oldest cedars. Hugging my body close to the bark as I had been taught. I came from a long line of hunters, well-schooled in the art of camouflage. I watched the girl silently. Waiting for the right moment to approach.

I was less enamored with her than the old ones. Rest assured, I had my reasons to be cautious. Humans were tricky creatures. Not to be trusted. They pulled out metal weapons that stole the souls of animals and hid traps with jaws that ripped the limbs off cubs. Leaving a wolf to die without honour.

There were wolves who believed the humans could be turned. But I had seen enough of the world to know otherwise. I kept a close eye on any man, woman, or child that entered our territory. Especially the ones with a pretty disguise and careless ways.

The Red One was just old enough to exert her will yet young enough not to feel responsible. Those humans were the most dangerous, for they wielded power without skill.

Somehow, their parents grew to believe this was a wiser way for their cubs to learn the ways of the world. Stumbling through the same mistakes their elders had made. Instead of teaching them wisdom and passing down the knowledge of their clan.

And so their young ones wandered the world without direction, without purpose, and worst of all, without a sense of responsibility. So I did not share the sense of hope that the cedars insisted on whispering to my highly tuned ears. No. Instead, I was suspicious. Wondering what game she played.

I watched as the Red One swung around another tree. Unaware of my presence. That did not give me comfort. If anything, her oblivion made me doubt her more. But I had been sent on this errand. I must fulfill my role. Though I was in a fouler mood than usual to deal with a human today.

My brother had gone missing. And I feared the worst. The humans in the local villages were on the warpath. Convinced that each time a sheep went missing or a chicken got eaten that it was one of our kind. Assuming we were as lazy as vultures.

Did they not know we preferred a fair fight? I glared at the girl. My fur stood up on my hackles. Their first assumption is always that we have no honour. They never see that they leave us no choice when they steal our lands. Forcing us further and further into a tiny patch of woods.

The smaller the woods became, the less we had to feed our families. Our clans barely existed on squirrels and groundhogs. The humans starved our kind until we had no choice than to hunt the large game they foolishly kept in open pens. We knew it was dangerous to approach their lands, but we took the risk to keep our cubs alive.

I sighed as I watched the foolish girl. Why me? It was not my place to ask. The grandmother had spoken. She saw the Red One in a vision and declared that she was the savior. I growled silently, not wanting to contradict my elders. But not believing that this girl had more than fleeting, careless thoughts between her tiny pink ears.

No sooner had the notion passed from my mind, than the Red One appeared right in front of me. Her feet planted firmly. Her eyes staring into mine without hesitation. The fur raised on my back. Every muscle in my body quivered with the impulse to lunge at her. It took all my strength to hold back.

No one sneaks up on a hunter and confronts her face on! Did this girl know nothing? But strangely, she was not afraid. The Red One crouched down and gazed at me. I could tell she wanted to touch my face, but was wise enough to sense my resistance. She kept her hands by her sides. And simply held me in her mind.

Though she restrained her hands, she did not hold back her feelings. The moment she bent her knees, she decreed silently that I was her sister. Staring deep into my eyes, the Red One proclaimed her love for me without so much as knowing my name.

5

The love that flowed from her heart was overwhelming. I had not felt such unconditional acceptance since I was a pup. And my warrior heart wrestled with the tenderness of such expression. I could not afford to feel this! What was she doing to me? This child must be a witch. A spellcaster. A traitor sent to infiltrate my clan!

As much as my resistance wished that to be true, my heart knew these were lies. The same lies told about wolves for centuries. This girl was of my kind, only without the fur and fangs. She was one in the same as my heart. She was my kin.

I struggled and cringed and fought with these feelings. The recognition of a kindred spirit. My mind filled with flashes of lifetimes spent as spirited pups born of the same pack. Then hunters of the same tribe fending off desecration of our land. Still others as sisters burned at the stake for our belief in the ancient ways.

I had no control over what was happening. A terrifying thought for a hunter of my rank. I felt the Grandmother's presence, and her voice whispered, *"Let go."* And I knew she had chosen me for this task. No other was meant to be here.

In the moment of release, a deep need to be with this girl… at her side…tore open my heart and swore me to her everlasting service in the blink of a heron's eye.

I could not hold it in any longer. I tipped my head back and howled. A howl that echoed through the farthest reaches of the canopy. Sending chills up the spines and down the roots of the old ones. A howl that declared my allegiance to the Red One.

Carried on the wings of ravens, the message made its way to the Grandmother that the pact had been made. Just as she had foretold.

◆◆◆

As I stared into the elegant wolf's eyes, I knew I had made the right choice. Though my mind had screamed at me not to approach the wild animal, my heart knew I had to be with her. She was calling to me. Or maybe her heart was. For her eyes were suspicious, and even filled with hate, but her heart. Oh, her heart called out to mine.

Whispering names we had not used for one another in centuries. Sister. Soulheart. Kindred spirit. Familiar. Names that caused a chill to go up my spine, and seized my mind, for fear of being tied to a stake and burned. Those days were not so far behind us that they could not be repeated.

But my heart would not be denied. And so, in the flash of a second, I had launched myself before the regal animal. Knowing that if she did not share my feeling, she would devour me. Tearing out my throat. Doing the deed I longed for but lacked the courage to do myself. Ending the heartache of this world and sending me back home.

That dark dream was not to be. She raised her hackles and the thought crossed her mind. I felt the instinct flood her muscles like an ancient call to battle. But a deeper promise, to one called The Grandmother, held her back. She revered this being. And would not put the whims of her own needs above the commitment she had made.

After her howl sent chills through the woods, and my heart, she turned. She was waiting. The time had come for her to take me to her elders. I hesitated. Was I ready? What did this mean? Would I ever go home again? The fears flooded my mind. And still, she waited.

Suddenly, I knew. The fears no longer mattered. I had leaped. And here we were. There was no turning back from this path. No matter where it led. Or how frightening the turns in the darkness might be.

I touched my hand to her back, acknowledging silently that

we were, again, one. She turned her head and set off into the depths of the woods. Trotting at a pace that allowed me to stay by her side but was far from her natural rhythm had she been able to run free.

Somehow, I sensed that time was of the essence. So I picked up my pace. Running as quickly as I could without tiring too soon. I had no idea how far we were travelling, but I knew The Grandmother was not to be found on the edge of the woods.

As we moved together, deeper and deeper into the trees, we covered paths I had never set foot on. My mind screamed with fear, but my heart knew this was the right way. We were on a mission that I could not deny. Even if it meant I was gone for days and my teachers sent scouts looking for me, this was a path I had to take.

By now, they were used to my errant ways. Disappearing in the evening and sometimes skipping class to wander the woods without supervision. The sisters would chide me and tell me not to risk the darkness of the wild woods. For evil animals lurked behind the tall trees, waiting to eat foolish young ones such as me.

I knew they warned me from their own heart-clenching beliefs. Desperate to keep me in the confines of a civilized world, they insisted on order. The kingdom of God had no room for wildness. Or abandon. And certainly no place for creatures of fur, feather, and bone. Their kingdom barely included women, let alone wolves.

But I did not want that education. I longed for the songs of birds and the symphonies of forests. Leaves rattling with the rhythm and languages of old. Howls of the heart. These were whispers I understood, and yearned for like a lover lost on the wings of ancient winds.

I did not belong in these strange last days of the nineteenth century. Filled with wars and obsession and rabid men with delirious dreams of owning the whole world. I belonged in the wild, with the ones that remembered where we once all belonged.

The days of the garden were not so long ago, if we chose to pay attention. I knew this as truly as I knew my hair was red. I had surrendered to the beauty of the beast. The wonder of the wild. And that was the true reason the sisters feared for my soul. But I could not change my heart any more than I could change who I was.

Instantly, I flashed back to the present. Senses on full alert. We were being followed. Despite that we had travelled miles into the deep darkness of the woods, there was a man on our heels. I reached out to feel what he wanted. Men were typically easy to read. They broadcast their urges as clearly as a dog in heat.

But this one was clever. He concealed his intention. I could not sense what he wanted. And that made me frightened – for both of us. There was only one thing to do. Confront him.

I stopped, suddenly. My sister responded as though we were one. She whirled and put her body in front of mine. Hackles up. She growled and scanned the woods for our pursuer. Sensing him close by but unable to pinpoint his location.

I longed to touch her coat; to connect us and acknowledge her fierce protection. But the gesture would throw her off her game. So I used my skills. Growing very still, I sought the location of this man. This hunter. Seeking out his beating heart. The quiet *thud thud thud* that betrayed every living being. The pulse that could not be denied.

And with that knowledge, I looked straight up into the branches of the great cedars. Spotting him in an instant. Just in time for my sister to knock me backwards with a swing of her body. As the arrows he sent flying hit the ground where I had stood.

"What do you want?" I hurled at him. "We have done you no harm!"

"So you say," he threw back.

9

Launching down in a swift motion to land on the ground in front of us. My sister growled. Keeping him from approaching.

But the Hunter was bold. In the blink of an eye, he pulled an arrow, set the bow, and aimed the sharp point at my heart.

"Take me to the one you call, Grandmother," he demanded. "Or I will pierce her heart and sell it at the market to the highest bidder."

"No one wants my heart," I declared. For this had been the truth of my life.

"You are wrong," the Hunter sneered. "Many a man will pay to eat the heart of a witch."

Turning his hate-filled gaze on my kin, he added, "And her familiar."

I felt his spine-chilling hatred fill the air. His fingers itched to release the arrow. Only his deeper need to reach The Grandmother kept him from killing me on the spot.

"Some seek it for the delicate taste," he explained. "And others believe your heart contains mystical powers. Either way, I make a handsome wage."

I felt the dilemma in my sister's heart. Betray me or betray The Grandmother. Neither was a choice she wanted to make. And so, I stepped forward and put my heart against his arrow. Making the choice for her.

"Do your worst," I whispered. Looking straight into his eyes. Meeting the darkness with my will.

The Hunter grinned. Dark thoughts of rampage and rape poured into his mind. Not caring whether his raging desires dampened the magic of my heart. He did not believe in old wives' tales. But he could not say whether the ones who did might guess what he had done.

His cruel eyes locked on mine. His body pressed forward, but his fingers held still. The Hunter's conflicting desires gave my sister long enough to act. She tilted her head back and howled.

Sending a call for help through the farthest reaches of the forest. Within seconds, flashing eyes and glinting teeth surrounded us. Growls echoed from behind multiple trees.

Knowing he was surrounded, the Hunter lifted his arm higher as though to announce his intent to pierce my heart should any creature come closer.

"I hear you are looking for me," a regal voice spoke behind him.

The Hunter turned as far as he could without relinquishing his angle; and came face to face with The Grandmother. Her presence glowed in the center of the woods, like the full moon at the height of harvest. And her silver coat reflected the wisdom of her years.

She was not afraid of the Hunter. Her confidence rippled through the hearts of her clan. Bringing the wolves out from the shelter of the trees, and into a tight circle around us.

As much as the Hunter wanted my heart, his hatred for the wolf pack was stronger. These wild devils had stolen his son, sending him into a dark pit of despair. Never to see daylight again.

Until, one day, the alluring voice of vengeance spoke to him. Promising him peace if only he conquered the one they called, The Grandmother. As they had pierced the heart of his clan, so would he take the heart of theirs.

Then he would know tranquility. Even if it cost him his life.

And so, the Hunter turned his arrow from my heart to The Grandmother. Aiming the point between her eyes.

"Your life or the girl's," he announced.

"And if I choose neither?" Grandmother replied.

"A debt must be paid," the Hunter growled back. "Choose."

"Your son," she said, sagely.

"He was but three years old!" the Hunter yelled, his hand shaking. "I will never consider it a fair exchange."

"Your owner, the King of Prussia, would," she spoke quietly.

"For he set the price of your son's head."

The Grandmother paused. And let her words ring through the forest.

"You crossed his will too many times," she continued. "Taking as many pelts as your greed desired. Stealing them from his lands without permission."

She stood, serenely. Speaking words he needed to hear out loud. "A bargain was struck for our protection from your wanton bow," she said. "The King insisted that I must be the huntress to take your child. A brutal exchange, to be sure, but a choice I had to make to protect my pack."

The Hunter's bow quivered. He knew she spoke the truth. He had taken wantonly all his life. Believing his clever ways lined his pockets without the knowledge of the authorities. Always thinking he was smarter than everyone else.

Until the day he came home, shoulder laden with pelts, and discovered blood and torn sheets in his son's bed. He fell to his knees and called out in pain. But there was no one to hear him. His wife was long gone.

The child had been the only thing holding her in his possession. She must have stepped away, only to return to an empty nest. With her beloved child dead, she held no allegiance to her husband. She fled within moments.

"And now I see," The Grandmother added, "that the King played us both. Knowing full well this day would come. That you would seek vengeance. And we would exterminate each other."

She waited for the Hunter to hear what she was saying. They had each been placed on the altar of the powerful. The ones who believed they owned every creature that walked the earth. And drew pleasure from reminding others of their control.

"Walk away," she whispered softly. "This is not the path to peace. This is the way of nightmares. If you take my pelt, you only seal the pain in deeper. Relinquish this debt. And we will both be free."

"I care not for your bargains," he declared, desperately clinging to his quest. Hands shaking, he readied the arrow for his claim. His crazed mind had envisioned this too long. He could see no other path to salvation.

"But you do," I said, stepping forward. Locking eyes with The Grandmother, I sought her permission to intercede. She felt the intention of my heart. The instinct coursing through my veins. And though she did not wish to place me in harm's way or relinquish her role as protector of the pack, she nodded.

"You long for release from your prison. A cell of your own making."

I paced around him. Feeling the old ways rush through my body. Acting purely from instinct, I opened to a voice as old as the trees bearing witness to our exchange.

Casting forth an enchantment, as I walked 'round and 'round. Feeling the earth sending her power through me. Sensing the protection of the ancient cedars. My brethren must have felt it, too.

The wolves fell silent and locked ranks in a circle.

Standing in allegiance, with The Grandmother at their crown, they watched as I wove my words around this man. Freeing myself of all that had come before me, to allow all that might come through me.

"You are not the man who entered this woods," I chanted. Eyes locked on his. Seeing past his hatred, to the ache underneath.

"You are a new man," I spoke softly, as my words touched the core of his heart. "Freed from the curse of old hurts. Freed from the pain of your lonely heart."

I stopped and opened my arms wide. Facing my heart toward his heart. Leaving my chest wide open to the sharp point of his arrow.

This was the moment he could seize my life. I was ready for such a sacrifice.

Every wolf in the circle held her breath. And I released the life that had come before me. Not knowing who would be the one to win, I took the leap of faith.

"Fall to your knees," I whispered. The Hunter dropped to his knees.

"Drop your bow," I declared. The Hunter let his bow and arrow fall.

I fell to my knees before him. Face to face with the hunter who had killed my brethren. Eye to eye with my sworn enemy. Smelling the blood on his hands.

Still, I knew there was only one way to ease his pain and break the curse of revenge.

"Offer your heart to the woods," I asked. Knowing that this gesture must be made from his own free will. He must choose. I could not demand this of him. Or the curse would not be broken.

The Hunter stared at me. And I knew, he could still take my life with his bare hands. If he chose the path of hatred, my time was over. And the curse would win the day.

His hands raised slowly. I watched. Offering my neck to his whim. A tear fell down his cheek as his hands turned and locked one on top of the other. Resting over his heart.

My pulse raced. As surely as I was ready to die, this was not the death I expected.

As he offered his heart, I must offer mine. Sacrifice for sacrifice. Offering for offering. This was the way it was. This was the way it always must be.

My heart pounded. As I leaned in, and placed my lips on his. Locking my heart with his heart. Seeking his soul with my kiss.

I asked, humbly, for his forgiveness.

The woods stood silent. Waiting. Watching. The Hunter returned my kiss, sending forth his release. Placing his hands on my face. Acknowledging that love had won.

As he released me, and stared at my face as though he had not seen me until this moment, the Hunter let loose his anguish in a howl that racked the hearts of every being within earshot.

Freed from his burden, he crumpled to the ground. I placed a hand on his back, and held his head in my lap. Bearing witness to years of pain.

The Grandmother nodded, and disappeared as silently as she had come. Her pack followed, including my soul sister. She gave me one last look, to say we would see each other again. Then she returned to the depths of the woods.

Leaving me with the man who sought our grace. The man who had given me his heart. Knowing he was now my responsibility.

# BLOOD RED

## KATHRYN COTTAM

THE GIRL IS COVERED IN BLOOD.

It stains her hands, knees, and calves. There is a solitary smear of it across her right cheek as though one bloody finger bumped along that pale flesh while tucking aside a stray strand of long red hair. There is more blood on her skirt and coat, but the deep crimson of the wool camouflages whatever drops found their way there. She sits on the front step of the house, her arms locked about her chest, her chin tipped towards her collar bones, rocking as though to comfort herself. Strange sounds emanate from her throat. She will be taken from here to a tiled room and be stripped of her red coat and skirt, white blouse, tennis socks and running shoes. Her hands will be photographed. The blood on her fingers will be swabbed. The grit under her fingernails is headed for a microscope. Her fingerprints will no longer belong to her alone. They will be bathed in black ink and captured on a white bureaucratic form. She now belongs to the system. And when all of this is finished, someone will take more photographs. This is the start of a very long night. My partner has confirmed her identification, informed me she's married, in her mid-twenties; but right now she looks no more than a frightened child. As though the world she once knew has proven itself to be no more than a lingering childhood fairy tale.

She's either a magnificent actress or her shock is real.

My partner and I are first on scene. We are originally called to a break and enter two miles up the road. But when we arrive, that house is secure and the owner is annoyed; *I didn't call no police,* he grumbles. We do a walk-though regardless, finding nothing of course and are about to head back to town when the next call comes in. An apparent 10-96, but the dispatcher speaks with a soft catch in her voice. I get it. Neither my partner or I believe it. This town has never had a murder. It's a rural posting. Aside from the chicken farm, logging, and tourism, there isn't much here. For the most part the job consists of rounding up those who drink too much, speed too much, beat their wives too much. With the occasional summer boating accident that involves booze, bikinis and a one way trip to the bottom of the deepest lake in the province. *Another false call,* my partner growls. I don't mind, though. The anticipation of such a call, allows me to rehearse my training, at least in my head. Anyway, it beat sitting in the office tapping out tombstone information on a keyboard, writing occurrence reports, or shooting the shit with a Staff Sergeant who wanted to relive the good ol' days when you could lay down a beating without being hauled before a review board. I pull up the long curving dirt road that is the driveway to a clearing where a house stands. It is one of the older properties that line the lake; a one story rambling rancher made of wood and glass. Old money. I bet the view from the back of this place — in the light of day — is stunning; it would have an unimpeded view of the water. I radio dispatch that we've arrived and park next to a large hollow stump. Together, my partner and I step out of the vehicle.

The girl is seated on the front stairs.

In the dark all we can see is the pale moon of her face — white and still. As we approach a motion sensor light flares in the dark, lighting the space where she sits and trembles.

And we see the red. So much of it. It takes a minute to realize that her coat and skirt are the same colour as the blood on her hands. Her hands. In one is a cell phone still connected to the 911 operator, and in the other, a bread knife. She holds it out in front of her, as though for protection. But her hand shakes with such palsy, that she could protect no one. Least of all herself. Her eyes are unfocused and my partner has to tell her several times to drop the knife. The phone falls first. Then the blade. I ask her name. But she is unable to answer, still in shock. My partner asks if there is anyone else in the house. She shakes her head. Then says, yes. Gran. And the tears fall.

My partner indicates he is going to clear the house. I nod as he disappears within, and taking the girl by her thin arm, lead her to the car. I open the rear door, and seat her inside. Then I go into the trunk, unzip my duty bag, find a tin of peppermints. I take one out. I know what's coming. The smell of decomposition — it gets in your nose, your mouth, your lungs. I place a peppermint on my tongue — it will help to mask the sting of death…I rezip my duty bag, seal the trunk.

I glance in the rear window. The girl's hands are folded in her lap, her head forward, hair falling, obscuring her face. There isn't a sound from her.

When my partner returns his face is as pale as the girl's. He nods. Then stumbles over to the edge of the drive and vomits. When he's finished we change places.

I enter the house and walk the hallway to the back of the house where a large bedroom is located. I stop before entering the room, take out my notebook and map my route. When finished, I peer inside. The bed is against the far wall. And the old woman lies in the middle of once white sheets that are now stained with red. Her eyes are wide with surprise or fright. Her lips are pulled back in death's grimace. Her white hair is tangled about the ruinous flesh that was once her throat. Blood has pooled across

21

the floorboards, sprayed across the ceiling, stained the walls. I retrace my steps down the hall, and out to the dark of the night, and the cool air. I rejoin my partner at the car.

Neither of us say a word.

As we stand there in silence, there is a knock on the car window. I reach down and open the door.

Her white face looks up at us. The smear of blood — now looks black as though a piece of the night has settled on her skin.

"I didn't do it," she says.

And then the three of us wait in silence until the sirens announce the arrival of a day without end.

◆◆◆

My partner borrows a car from another member and returns to the detachment with the girl to begin the forensic process. I remain behind to manage the exhibits. I am careful to record everything as it's photographed, gathered, labelled. There's the girl's phone, the knife, the sheets, the kettle, the broken glass, the brick, and the list goes on. What isn't there is the weapon that killed the old woman. Patrol searches the house, the grounds, along the highway but the weapon is not located. Eventually, I leave the lake — and the buzz of activity at the lake house — and drive back alone to the detachment.

The road is quiet; it will be dawn soon. The night is just now shrugging off the last vestige of sleep and soon daylight will be stretching her sunlit fingers across the horizon.

Curious, I drive by the girl's address...It's a hard-knock house on one of the poorer streets in town. A marked difference to the old woman's place. A shit-brown buick skylark sits on a small patch of concrete that must have once been grass. The house is box-shaped, with peeling paint, and an eave that has fallen to the ground, so that it looks like the house is resting her head upon this one thin slice of metal. There is an open window and a thin pink curtain flutters in the morning breeze…I yawn. Hit the accelerator.

When I next see the girl she is no longer dressed in red. Now her hands are clean. Scrubbed free of blood and ink. She wears a white paper suit that covers her from toe to neck. A bunny suit, we call it. There is a can of coke at her elbow, along with a cold fast food  hamburger still in its wrapper. We sit across from one another in an interview room specifically designed to be uncomfortable. The lights are bright, her chair, metal and specifically designed to wobble. It's cold in here. I apologize for the temperature. But in truth, it's deliberately set to be chilly. We've been through her story once, thrice, seven times now. It never wavers.

I ask her about the knife she was holding when we arrived. She grabbed it from a drawer in the kitchen; terrified that he — whoever did this — would return. I know it's not the weapon we are looking for. For one, there was no blood on that knife, at least not the blade. There would be trace amounts on the handle, transferred there from her own fingers. But the Coroner has already told us that the weapon that killed the old woman was most likely an axe; dogs were now searching the roadway but I doubt they would find it; whoever killed the old woman took it when they left.

As day approaches I know she is still holding back. When asked if she knows anyone who would harm her husband's Gran, she hesitates. Takes a breath, bites one of those red lips and shakes her head. I ask her to answer aloud for the sake of the audio recorder. But her mouth and tongue won't — or can't — form the word: no.

I tell her I am tired, she is tired. And the longer she withholds the more likely her Gran's killer won't be caught. Finally, when dawn is about to break, so does she.

My HUSBAND — Jake — is drinking again, spoiling for a fight, yelling about money and bills. I try my best to keep us on budget. I do. Spend only what he give me. The rest of the money he looks after. But there's less of it each week, and more of the pills and drink. He wants me to pick up extra shifts at the cafe. But I am working as many shifts as Brian can give me; it wouldn't be fair to them other girls if I were to take them all. There aren't a whole lotta jobs in town at this time of year, you see. In summer, it's different. The lakeside swells with tourists and all the shops and restaurants need extra hands. But in winter? Pickings are few. And Jake starts demanding I go back to the factory. It's true, they like me there. I'm a hard worker. But I can't. The chicken feathers — you see, they get in your mouth, your throat. You cough and spit white feathers into the air. And the birds. They scream when death comes, you see. It's not a quiet thing. And the blood — you can taste it on the air. It made me near-mad. I had to quit. But Jake don't understand. All he can see is the money. He says he'll talk to Darryl — my old foreman — tomorrow; see if they'll take me back on. I get angry, say something I shouldn't. What do I say? Do I have to? Very well. I say, the Doctor says his back is better now; so why can't he go back to cutting wood? Instead of sitting on the couch drinking beer, swallowing pills and flipping between trashy sport channels... And that's when he — I won't go back to the factory. I just won't. I'm sorry. Do you have tissue? Thank you... I hate crying. It makes me feel weak. Jake hasn't had it easy, you see. His parents died in a car accident when he was in grade six (his father's drinking to blame, so said his Gran). She took him in after they died, raised him up. But Gran says

Jake has too much of his father's blood in him and the drink is a weakness in that family. Among the men, anyway. Which is why they have to marry strong women. But Jake's father had no such luck; he married a woman weaker than he. And here, Jake's Gran would always sniff with resentment; as to whether it was because Jake's mom was a simpleton or because she failed to keep her husband from driving the car that night, I dunno. Anyway, I'm sorry, I'm rambling again. I always liked Jake at school, but when I met his Gran — sometimes I wonder if I married him for her. I never had a mom, you see. She lit out when I was three, leaving Pop and me alone. I think that's what made me like Jake. Neither of us had a mom. But he had a Gran. And whenever I was over, she'd give me a hug — she smelled like roses and old furniture polish — and I never wanted to leave. And later, when things got bad between the two of us — Gran always insisted I come to the lake house and stay with her — she wouldn't let me return until he apologized. So that's what I did tonight. I went — slipping out of our bedroom window — quiet so as not to disturb Jake. If he found me — well, I always have to be sure he don't. I caught the number seven bus across town to the last stop. Yes, I think the bus driver will remember me. I was crying and he asked if I was alright. You know, in high school everyone would tell me I was so pretty; that of all of us I would escape this town and make something of myself. But I was smart too. Good with math and science and literature. I think that used to surprise people. I coulda done anything, gone anywhere. I even had a scholarship to a college out of state. But, Jake. By then I was in love with him. And he was following his father's footsteps into logging, and we were talking marriage. And I got pregnant. You don't know about that? Yeah. I lost the baby. Etopic pregnancy. That made Jake hard. He kept saying I done something to cause it. Even though the Doctor said it wasn't my fault. And then the accident — and he started drinking more. And I don't mind the booze so much. It's the pills … sorry. I've forgotten your question. Could you please repeat it? Thank you. Yes, the walk was nearly an hour but there was no money for a cab and I've done it before. Besides, I'm very careful. If a car comes along, I step off the road and hide in the trees that line the highway. I'm not scared of the dark or the woods. But it's better not to be seen. Once Jake came after me. And well — it would have been best not to have been caught. No, I didn't see anyone as I approached. But Gran was home because the lights were on in the house. I knocked several times but she don't answer. Which was strange. I've turned up at all manner of hour of night and she always opens the door, gives me a hug, and puts me to bed with a dram of whisky. So this was very odd. I tried the front door, but it was locked. So I pushed my way through the brambles at the side of house (they tend to get overgrown come fall; and yes, that's what caused the scrapes and cuts on my calves), and climbed the wooden steps to the patio door.

That door was locked as well, but there is no curtain covering the glass window. I could see the kettle on the stove — taste the smell of burning steel — and knew it boiled dry. I knocked again, this time calling out for Gran. I even used both fists on the glass. But she don't come. I was worried. She had a pacemaker put in last year. I remember the heart doctor saying it ran on a battery. What if it gave out? Gran keeps a brick on the back step. We use it to prop open the door in the summer, let the lake breeze cool the house. So I picked it up and smashed the window. Then I reached through the broken glass — I guess that's when my fingers and arm got cut — and unlocked the door… Next? Do I have to? Alright…Well, I entered the house and first thing I did was switch off the stove. I used a towel to grab the kettle from the burner and throw it into the sink. It stank of steel, so I doused it with cold water. I remember the steam erupting in a volcanic frenzy. I remember the way my face broke out in sweat.

I called out for Gran. But still she don't answer. So I went to her bedroom.

There was so much blood. I tried to stop the bleeding. But it was too late.

◆◆◆

Please don't ask me to tell the story again. I no longer wish to see the blood. Very well.

Gran was lovely. Who would want to hurt her? This bruise? It's nothing. I've had worse. Yes, Jake has a temper but — he don't mean to hit me. I just make him angry sometimes. I should learn to keep my mouth shut. No, I suppose nobody asks to get hit. How? His right hand. Closed fist. Anyway, I don't want to talk about this anymore. Can I please go home now? Gran? No, I don't know who would do such a thing. Pardon? Jake would never hurt her. They may have argued of late, but he loved her. It was nothing, really. I shouldn't have said that. It wasn't so much an argument. It's just she disapproved of his drinking. You see his Gran is — was — wealthy. And when he was first injured, she helped out with some of the bills, is all. But then she saw the money was going to the drink and the pills and so she stopped giving him cash. I tried to tell Jake we don't need Gran's money. We were doing just fine. At least, we were before Jake lost his job and the benefits stopped. Where's Jake? At home, of course. He's always at home. No, of course, I wouldn't know if he followed me to Gran's. I don't see him once I leave. Yes, I supposed he could have been driving one of the cars that passed me on the highway. But I hid, remember? Besides he would never hurt his Gran. He loved her. Just like he loves me.

My partner had sent patrol to pick up the girl's husband and bring him in for an interview. I leave the girl now — telling her to remain seated — and go to watch my partner who is speaking with her husband. Whereas the girl looks young, he looks older than his years. Cigarettes have aged the skin of his face. His fingers are stained yellow. The muscles on his arms and belly giving way to fat. The stale smell of booze lingers in the hallway outside the room in which he is enclosed. I make my way to another office, to stand before the monitor and watch the interview.

I'm asleep on the couch when the goddamn cops start banging on the screen door. You'd think they'd open that metal piece of shit and apply their fists to the wood. But nope. Too fucking lazy. And so it sounds like metal thunder about to bring down the goddamn house. I wait for Red to get the door, but as usual her lazy ass doesn't make an appearance. Christ, I have to do everything around this joint. And I'm the one with the broken back. Not that she believes it. Even though a goddamned tree fell on me. A tree! It was the fault of the fucking tree-huggers. I was used to ripping up the ground with a tractor, but the big boss wanted some publicity photos, showing his boys cutting trees by hand. So there was Pete and I, chainsaws out. Calculating the lean of tree. Ensuring the fall path was clear. Making the face cuts.

But somehow Pete miscalculates. I get struck by one of the lower branches, knocked off my feet, land heavy on my back. Sometimes at night I can feel the weight of that tree pressing down on me. I can't breathe, can't feel my limbs, and so I chase the pain. Ah. There it is. And when the hurt returns, it's like a fucking drug. But at least I know I'm still alive, right? Red doesn't get it. Thinks I should be back at work by now. What's that? You wanna know about the old lady? Yeah, I went to the lake house tonight. 'Cause she called and fucking asked me to come, that's why. I dunno. Maybe she wanted to say sorry for being such a cold hearted bitch. Huh? 'Cause I'm on disability — the accident, remember? I tell you about that? Twice? Okay, fuck you — *I hate this metal chair. One leg is shorter than the other and every now and then it tips and I feel like I'm falling. Like that day in the woods* — What? I dunno, the old bat wasn't there. What? Were the lights on? I don't fucking remember. Okay, okay. Keep your panties on. Yeah. I guess the lights were on 'cause I switched off the car headlights. And I wouldn't have done that if it was all dark. I knocked, she don't answer, I go home. Good enough? What was the fight about? What fight? There was no fight. What did that bitch say? Well, that's true. She wouldn't give us no more money. You tell me how we're supposed to get by on Red's salary at the cafe? Bitch earns minimum wage and people around these parts don't tip worth shit. I got medical bills. Meds. That adds up, you know. When was my last drink? None of your goddamned business. Jesus, I need a smoke. What? Christ, who ever heard of a non-smoking cop-shop? After we talk? Fine. No, the old bat wasn't home. Or at least she never answered the door. What was I supposed to do? Fucking hang around all night waiting for the old biddy to answer the door? No, I don't try to get in. Last time I tried that, she called the fucking cops on me. Her own goddamned kin. Oh, you know about that? Yeah, well, we needed twenty bucks for some groceries. Twenty bucks! The old lady's rolling in it and she can't spare a double dime for some soup and crackers to keep her grandson's belly full? Jesus. Why you asking about Red? Bullshit. I never hit that woman in my life. I love her. Why would I do that? I know you fucking cops came to the house once. Okay, twice. 'Cause she's a fucking liar, that's why. She was pissed at me for getting fired when I refused to go back to work. With this fucking back? Doesn't matter the goddamned Doctor can't find nothing wrong; I'm in fucking pain all the time. What? I'm telling you! She was pissed, so she called the cops. The bruises? She's a goddamned klutz. Always knocking into walls and shit. What the fuck is this all this about anyway? My goddamned back is killing me. I need another chair. Okay, okay, I'll sit. Jesus Christ, no need to break out the fucking hardware. No, I don't see Red there. Why would I? She was asleep. I turned the car around and went home. No, I don't stop anywhere. It was midnight for fuck's sake. Where am I gonna go? The kitty stroll for some pussy? Have you seen the girls in this town? Jesus Christ, it's a joke. Don't you cops got no sense of humour? And, no, it's none of your goddamned business how much I drank last night. What the fuck is going on? Did that bitch say I hit her again? Maybe I goddamned should. Might knock some sense into that pretty little head of hers. Have you seen my wife? She's a goddamned cherry. Every man in this town wanted to fuck her. And I got her. What's that? Would I mind if detectives searched the car? Why the hell would they wanna do that? What do you mean the old woman's dead? I knew that fake heart wouldn't last. I told her as much. Not her heart? Jesus Christ. Someone took an axe to her? No fucking way. No fucking way can you look in my car. Not unless you have a goddamned search warrant. No fucking way.

THE SEARCH WARRANT doesn't take long to get. My partner has a knack with one particular judge.

I go next door to the other monitor — the one that is trained on the girl. Someone has brought her a coffee. Steam spirals from the cup, and touches her lips. She is still seated, hands tucked beneath her thighs. She looks exhausted. Spent. Drained. Things will never be the same. I go down the hall to the washroom and examine myself in the mirror. Dark hair with grey at the temples. Lines crease my forehead, the corners of my eyes. I'm in need of a shave. I wash my face and hands with cold water. I've been up for over twenty-four hours now; I need sleep. Or a break. The dreariness of my existence was temporarily broken by this case; but by the end of the week I will be back to my old routine. I've been here ten years now. Sent to this small town as punishment for a mistake I made when I was far younger. Back then, I was green. Scared all the time. But you couldn't let it show. Not to the man on the street. And definitely not to the partner that stood beside you. Cops find outlets for that fear in the usual places; booze, cigarettes, sex. I found it in a witness to a murder. She had been gentle and kind amidst the chaos, and I had sought comfort there. When discovered, the whole case unravelled. I was suspended. There was an investigation. But my inexperience saved me. And landed me here. Where if mistakes were made, less damage would be done. Where nothing ever happened, at least not until today. And the monotony of it all weighed far heavier than the fear ever had.

I make my way back to the interview rooms. Someone is

pouring out a fresh pot of coffee. I grab a mug and hold out the cracked ceramic for a fill.

*Wolfe,* our ident tech says, and I turn to see him standing there with a long, flat cardboard box. *Tossed in the back seat of the husband's car,* he says and lifts the lid. Inside, zap-strapped in place, is an axe spattered with blood.

*His clothes were in the trunk as well. Soaked through with blood. Don't know why he didn't toss them in the lake.*

*Well, if they were all smart, we'd be out a job,* another voice says. And those of us in the room laugh, in part, because we know it is true.

The ident tech seals the lid, and exits to congratulatory pats on the back. As my partner delivers the news to the husband and begins the charter process, I watch his face fall in shock, then tighten with resistance. His voice rises octave by octave as he proclaims his innocence. I drink the coffee in one long burning swallow.

Shift over.

◆◆◆

The girl is quiet as she sits in the back of the wagon. One of the jail guards found her a faded pair of jeans and a sweatshirt from a bunch of spares kept on hand. The jeans were several sizes too big for her and sat loose about her waist and hips. The sleeves of the sweatshirt were too long, falling well past her fingertips. Swallowed up in all that fabric she looks even younger than before. I pull up at the hotel, and park in the lot. Then I step out and release her from containment. She cannot return home; her house has been sealed until the search warrant can be processed. The department keeps an account here for emergency situations so checking her in is quick. I claim the keys from the desk jockey and walk her to a room on the second floor. It smells of stale air. Orange curtains hang on the far wall to disguise the fact that there is no window.

I close the door behind us and she throws her arms about my neck, pressing her slim body against mine.

My own arms wrap about her, but my grip is not as tight as hers. It never has been. She always laughs at me, teases me for thinking she will break.

"How was I?" she breathes in my ear.

"Perfect," I say, my voice gruff from questioning her all night, and then because I have been thinking about it since I left the lake house, "Did you have to use an axe?"

She laughs and her breath is hot and smells of bitter coffee.

"It somehow seemed appropriate," she smiles. "Everything go okay for you?"

I nod, it was easy enough to grab the axe from where she had placed it — wrapped in Jake's clothes — from the hollow log when I remained outside with her after my partner went to clear the house. All the while the search went on, the bloody thing was tucked in my duty bag. When the dogs arrived, it was my cue to leave. Jake's car was where she said it would be. Sitting on that patch of concrete outside the square house that comprised her existence. She had given me the spare keys to it the night before at the cafe and so it only took seconds for me to transfer the evidence from my trunk into the back seat.

"The keys?" she asked.

"Gone," I said. Disposed of down a sewer drain. As far as she knew, she would later tell the Judge, there was only one set. And those were found on Jake when he was arrested. His cries of —

*Goddamned Pussy Liar! Fucking —*

— would follow her out of the court house and onto the street.

"Good," she says and her shoulders relax. "You'll see. It's just as I said, Wolfe. The old lady was ridiculously wealthy. When we get the money we'll be able to do all we've ever dreamed of. We can go anywhere. Be anyone. Just like we imagined."

She takes my hand and draws me over to the bed, like she has so many times before in the shack out back of the cafe. The one hidden behind a patch of brush and weeds that hasn't seen a trimmer in years. At first the wooden hovel was filthy and so we used the wall for support. But soon, she started cleaning it, sweeping it free of cobwebs and bugs, washing the thick windows stained with grime so they would let in the light. Picking flowers so the space filled with the scent of spring daffodils. And then one night, half drunk, we put a mattress in there. A few blankets to keep it clean. From then on, I approached through the woods, she from the cafe. No one ever knows we met. Now, in this hotel, there is no one to hide from. I unlace my boots, kick them away. I lose my vest. Then she unbuttons my shirt, her fingers delicate and precise. I lift a hand to help, but she bats it away with surprising strength. Then she's releasing my belt. But this I want to do myself and when I drop it — gun, radio, handcuffs, baton, and more — to the floor, it feels like twenty pounds has been lifted from my shoulders. Now she's working the zipper of my pants. When the uniform is gone, and I am just me, she slides the borrowed jeans from her hips. Pulls the sweater from her naked breasts. She smiles again and climbs onto the bed, her red hair falling over her pale skin like slicks of blood. I close my eyes, shutting out the image of the old woman and her gory throat.

"Don't," she says, grabbing my hand, placing it against one cool breast, so that I can hear the beat of her heart. When I am able to look at her again, she releases my hand and I crawl over her, looking down at her head on the pillow.

She had such large eyes, such white teeth. And her hands on my forearm had such sharp claws.

Blood. It gets under your skin, in your mouth, on your tongue. You can taste it. Hear it. It sings to you, makes you mad.

She reaches up to pull my mouth down to hers, but I resist, mesmerized by her fingers; they are no longer stained but I can still see the blood.

# GIRL IN RED

**ROBERTA COTTAM**

HE SAW HER RED CLOAK before he saw her. Amidst the near-naked trees, their dark limbs bristled with the dry, yellow leaves of autumn, the garment's bright scarlet hue was impossible to overlook. It hung by its hood, hooked on a birch branch, its hem puddling on the mossy forest floor.

*Clever girl,* he thought, lowering his rifle and returning it to its holster. *Wouldn't do to be mistaken for a doe.* Her dress, the skirt speckled with mud, was also red, with a pattern of small pink cherries. A pink ribbon tied up her fawn-coloured hair.

He pushed aside the tree branches and waded out of the bush onto the trail.

She was startled by his sudden appearance and dropped a handful of wild raspberries at the edge of the path. "Oh!" she cried, scrambling to her feet. She licked the fruit from her lips; the juice on her mouth looked like the blood of a fresh kill. Her nostrils flared and her eyes darkened. "I didn't know you were there."

"Forgive my intrusion." He extended a hand. "I'm Jacob."

"You need not pardon yourself," she said stiffly. But she did not ask him what he had been doing, watching her from the bushes. She dried her berry-stained hands on her skirt and placed one in his, as soft as his was rough, but her name she withheld. Once he'd kissed the back of her hand, she pulled it away and reached for her red cloak, but his quick reflexes fetched it first.

"Allow me," he said. "The day is getting late." And he held it out to drape over her shoulders.

Instead, she snatched it from his grasp and flung it over one arm. "I don't feel the cold," she said defiantly, but her nipples showed otherwise. Jacob wondered how he'd offended her, and reconsidered his strategy.

"Let me offer my assistance. May I be your companion through the forest?" He scanned the woods around them. He was certain she traveled alone. And though he knew there were other hunters in the forest, he felt—in that moment—that *he* alone was in her vicinity. He took a step closer, towering over her small frame. "I recognize you miss, miss, but do not remember your name. Please remind me."

She looked up at him with narrowed eyes, then shook out the red cloak and pulled it over her shoulders. "I will not answer you, sir, for I do not know you—"

"Jacob," he reminded her. He straightened the red cloak on her shoulders.

"*Jacob,*" she repeated with a thin smile, pulling the red hood up around her face. It cast a rosy shadow over her cheeks, as though the sun had suddenly set and turned the sky pink. "I am bound for my grandmother's and mustn't be late." She turned her back to him. "And my grandmother would not be pleased to know I stopped in the woods to speak to a strange man."

"Better a man than a wolf," Jacob mumbled as she stooped to retrieve a picnic basket.

She looked at him sharply over her shoulder, settling the basket's handle into the crook of her elbow. "What did you say?"

Jacob grinned. "I said, better run on your way."

◆◆◆

He tracked her throughout the afternoon. At times, she dawdled. At other times, she hurried along the trail, her pace lively with youthfulness, which caused him to break out in a sweat. Jacob rolled up his sleeves and wiped his brow dry. The rifle banging against his shoulder blade annoyed him. Once he stopped to sip from a spring, but he nearly lost her in the few seconds he'd detoured, and so he did not stray from the trail again.

She made Jacob's job simple for she was easy to track: She stayed on the footpath, never venturing into the brush. But even had she, her vivid clothing and loud footfalls would have given her away. Truth told, she dressed and moved as though to demand attention. And for the best, Jacob thought, for there were many hunters in the woods, hungry for wolf blood and hell-bent for the King's prize. And though Jacob was always sure of his mark, he could not say so of the other hunters' twitching fingers.

Certainly, it would be unwise to appear too much like an animal in these woods, wolf or otherwise. Jacob understood the risk he himself took in blending into his surroundings, wearing a leaf green cloak draped over a jacket and leggings fashioned in leather. A regular Robin Hood, he mused. Perhaps a highwayman's life might be his future. He'd never taken the roadways that led away from the village. In fact, he'd barely stepped out of the woods where he'd spent his childhood.

But he was no highwayman. He was a hunter through and through. He came from a long line of stalkers and trappers and anglers. His grandfather's cottage was decorated with the kills of many generations: bear and wolf heads surveyed each room with cold, glass eyes.

As a boy, Jacob did not understand the pride a man feels in

41

overcoming a beast. For it is a primitive urge to provide for one-self and his family, and Jacob—whose childhood table was always laden with meat and his bed padded with furs—never knew the struggle to feed and clothe himself, let alone another. Not like his father's father, and his father before him.

And so when Jacob became a man and inherited his grand-father's cottage at the edge of the wood, he had little ambition for the kill. Instead, he chose to live simply, eating chicken and eggs instead of the venison of his childhood. He wore no furs or jewelry carved of antler. He owned no collection of pistols or bows, snares or catapults. The only weapon he possessed was his grandfather's favourite rifle, which the old man had clutched on his death bed and the reverend, reading the last rights, had to pry from his fingers.

Despite showing little interest in hunting, Jacob inherited a keen eye for tracking. His father noticed that, at an early age, Jacob skillfully followed rabbits to their holes and ducks to their nests come evening. Burrows of babies and nests of eggs were Jacob's favourite discovery and once found, he kept a watchful eye over them, returning often to leave piles of carrot tops or sprinkle pumpkin and sunflower seeds. Sometimes, if Jacob suspected that a fox had come sniffing, he would sit by for hours, waiting for the red-headed thief to appear, so he could shout at the top of his lungs and chase it away.

As Jacob grew taller and spent an increasing amount of time in the woods, his father taught him to shoot. "For defense, my son," his father explained, for a boy alone in the woods might easily run into a bear or a wolf. Jacob nodded solemnly, understanding; if he were not around, who would watch over the ducklings? Jacob agreed that it was imperative he stay alive. Having been handed his grandfather's rifle, Jacob proved himself his father's child by shooting an acorn off an oak branch, and thus the lesson was complete.

As Jacob became a man, his ability to provide guardianship improved. While rabbits and ducks retained Jacob's protection, he extended his wardship to hedgehogs and badgers and white-tailed deer. Indeed, there were many creatures which required his care and attention, and Jacob learned to use his rifle to deter curious predators by sending warning shots into the air.

But today, Jacob's gun was close at hand not merely to fire a warning. Today, Jacob was prepared to take life, should the occasion arise. The scent of his last kill still lingered in his nostrils.

And then, she stepped off the path and pushed her way into the bracken, as if something had suddenly caught her ear. From the picnic basket she carried, she removed a loaf of bread and began to pick off crumbs which she dropped on the forest floor. She disappeared into the brush and Jacob quickly followed, her trail of breadcrumbs marking the way. *Foolish girl,* he thought. *The birds will eat those in no time.*

She followed the sound of a stream, pushing through the woods all the way down to the water. When she came to the riverbank, she deposited the picnic basket on a rock and removed her red cloak. Her lips retained a raspberry shadow, but it was washed away when she bent over the water to drink. She drank long and deeply, as though she'd not had water in a fortnight. Refreshed, she threw back her head and water cascaded down her chin and the front of her dress. She examined the wet fabric with dismay, plucking it away where it clung to her small, firm breasts. In an instant, she'd stripped off her wet bodice, shrugged out of her skirt and was standing naked on the riverbank. Jacob, unseen, shrank back into the bushes, his eyes locked upon her.

There was a girl in town he'd once watched in this way. Emily, she was called. She had raven-black hair and a rather thin nose, like a beak. But her voice was anything but a rook's; she sang and played a harp every evening at the rear window of her father's bakery, the yeasty aroma of rising bread escaping on the wind. Sometimes she came to the window freshly bathed, settling the harp into her lap dressed only in a nightgown, her long dark hair wet and clinging to her shoulders. And though he never saw the baker's daughter naked as he now did the girl in red, he knew every dimension of her body thanks to the hours he'd dedicated to observation: the exact weight of her footstep as she came to the window; the length of each finger as it plucked one of the instrument's strings; the precise pitch of her voice, sometimes tight and off-tune if she had not yet taken her evening peppermint tea.

Not once did Emily in her nightgown know that Jacob, the boy from the woods, perched outside her room in the limbs of an apple tree. How could he reveal himself? She lived a cultured life in town, educated in language and watercolours and seldom wearing the same dress from one season to the next. Jacob, on the other hand, had never read a book or sung a hymn or worn a suit that wasn't fashioned of buckskin.

With no money to take a bride, he stayed hidden in the apple branches. But how Jacob regretted it; one day, the smithy's son left a branch of apple blossoms on her windowsill. By the time apple pies sat cooling in the bakery window, she'd taken the smithy's name.

Jacob stepped out from his cover and ground his heel into the pebbles along the river bank to announce his presence, but the girl had already sensed him. She spun around the second he moved, shamelessly naked, and glared at him. Her skin shone as white as the moon. Then she ran into the water and dove under the current.

Jacob walked over to her scattered belongings on the bank. She surfaced and watched as he spread her damp bodice on a rock to dry and neatly folded her skirt, setting it aside. Then, he chose another rock upon which to sit, and helped himself to her picnic basket.

"That is for my grandmother," she barked from her place in the stream, only her head and shoulders visible above the waterline.

Jacob held a tempting apple tart under his nose. He sniffed the sweet dessert. "So you say," he mused, unconvinced. Then he rummaged deeper into the picnic basket. Ah, ha—meat! Kidney pie and salted fish and pork sausage. He held up a link of sausage. "For your grandmother, too?"

She sulked in the river, combing her fingers through her wet, tangled hair. "You may have *one*."

As Jacob bit the end off a sausage, she waded ashore, unabashed. He tossed her the red cloak which she used to dry herself and wrap around her bare skin while she warmed herself in the waning sunlight. Then she wriggled into her skirt and damp bodice as Jacob watched unapologetically, all the while chewing and swallowing, chewing and swallowing. He struggled to make sense of her. He had witnessed no beast quite like her.

Red hugged the cloak tightly around her shoulders and came over to where he perched on the rock. Her lips were tinged with blue. The day was coming to its end, the air cooling off. Jacob glanced up as the sun fell behind the tree-line. Not long and the first star would be visible. As though reading his thoughts, she said, "The dinner hour will soon be past. I must hurry on my way."

But Jacob knew she would not arrive at her grandmother's before dark, let alone the dinner hour. He passed her the picnic basket. "Yes, you mustn't keep your grandmother waiting." He watched for a response, a flicker of suspicion in her eye, a flush of colour in her cheek. Her face gave away nothing, as pale and blank as the moon at its fullest. Then he said, "I shall escort you back to the path."

She frowned and opened her soft red mouth to say

something, but she suddenly saw that the breadcrumbs were gone. "I'm sure I can sniff out my way," she pouted, pushing into the brush and scrambling over fallen branches and logs. The picnic basket banged against her shins.

Jacob put a hand on her elbow to steady her, the bones of her arm as frail as a bird's wing. He smiled to himself. She was stronger, he was sure, than she seemed. He led her away from the river, through the woods and back to the footpath. And when her feet were upon it, and he knew she would bolt, he quickly snatched up her hand and held it to chest. His heart hammered against her palm. He held her in his gaze, unwavering. "Best you go carefully," he said, still holding onto her fast. If only he could keep her in range, not only in sight.

She pursed her lips, saying nothing, looking like a vixen caught by a hound. When he finally released her hand, she whirled around and ran down the path, her red cloak fluttering behind like the red tail of a fox.

◆◆◆

The moon was up, a plump breast hanging in the sky, one side slightly cast in shadow. Last night's moon had been full, and his work easily done. Tonight would be different. Without a full moon, there would be no certainty. No proof. Still, the ample light shed through the tree branches aided his progress.

Though she'd begged haste at the riverside, she did not hurry along the path. And when the footpath dipped into a glen, the tree coverage whittling away into a grassy field laced with silver willows, she stopped. Jacob hid himself behind the large stump of a fallen tree. She set down the basket and helped herself to a pie—whether apple or kidney, he could not tell. She ate ravenously, wiping her sticky mouth on the folds of her red cloak. Then, she lay back in the tall grass and dipped her hand beneath her skirt.

Jacob's own stomach growled with hunger and another organ, too, stirred at the sight. The urge to watch was powerful, but he looked away, scanning the distant trees for distraction, hoping to spy a barred owl; it was the time of year they roosted in these parts.

There were no owls to distract him, and every tissue of his body begged him to peek. Yet it was not his place to watch this intimate act. He had watched such intimacy before: the mating of swans, the birth of a fawn, the death of an old badger.

But his body had not yearned in those moments as it did now.

Still, he gave only his ears the permission to become attuned to her act, keeping his eyes on the sky, the stars, the moon. He listened to her panting, intent on identifying some logical tune in the chaos of her fevered gasps. Her vocal chords vibrated as might the strings of a harp, and sounded like the keening of a doe whose fawn is felled by a bear. Perhaps he was in error.

The thought struck him like a punch—what if the girl-in-red did not wail in bliss, but in battle? But no, it could not be. He'd never raised his rifle in error before. There was no danger in these woods. Not anymore.

That moment, she howled like a dog, and as she did, a twig snapped nearby. A predator after all? Jacob refocused his eyes on the clearing: Red was barely visible behind the tall grass, and as her body bucked with pleasure, her tied-up hair flicked above the grass line like the switching of a wolf's tail. And not ten yards away from Jacob, a dark figure crouched at the edge of the field, mistaking the girl for a beast and raising a rifle.

How Jacob could not have seen the hunter was beyond comprehension. He remembered the day under the oak tree when his father had taught him to shoot. He'd thrust a finger in Jacob's gut. "This, son," he'd said, "is your greatest weapon out here in the woods. Before you hear a mountain cat, smell a bear or see a wolf, you must sense its presence. For otherwise, it is too late."

And Jacob had grown to understand every fibre of his being, the way his muscles tensed or how the hairs stood up on his neck when danger approached. And yet he'd been unaware of the other man. Something about Red confused his instinct.

As much as he loathed to admit, he had ignored his gut before, not all that long ago. A month past, he'd been walking through the village at a rather late hour, when he heard a beautiful sound. He knew it at once. Emily. He crept around to the back of the blacksmith's home and hunkered in the shadows. There she was at the window, a new baby in her arms that once had held a harp. She sang a lullaby and looked up at the full moon.

Jacob wanted to stay at her side. Indeed, something primitive called him to keep vigil. But it was not right: the child was not his, and Emily was another man's wife. His heart ached as he walked away. But not so much as it ached come the morning when he learned that both mother and child were dead, having been dragged from the building, mauled to their deaths and discarded in the woods.

And now, it had happened again—Jacob had turned away in propriety despite an urgent desire to stand watch. He knew he should have kept his eyes on the glen—his body had told him so, but he had not listened.

The crouching hunter cocked the hammer of his rifle, but Jacob was already moving darting across the open and field and wrestling the man to the ground. The bounty hunter fired, desperate to claim the king's ransom, but Jacob cranked the barrel of the gun skyward, sending the bullet overhead. The empty cartridge dropped at their feet like a nut from a branch.

The hunter swore at Jacob and spit in his eye, but Jacob delivered a punch to the jaw, overpowering his opponent. The man crumpled to the ground and was still. Jacob picked himself up and dusted off his hands.

He expected the girl to have fled, but she had been watching nearby. She drew closer, wide-eyed. "Are you hurt? Is he—" she asked, one hand touching her trembling lip. In the night, her fair hair looked almost as dark as Emily's. Her heaving chest reminded him of the way Emily's breath used to inflate her breast as she sang.

"He is only out cold. But he'll awake soon enough, so you best be on your way." If he were going to have her to himself, Jacob would have to keep in closer range. Thanks to the King's reward for the capture of Emily and her baby's killer, a hunt was on; anything that remotely appeared like a wolf would incite gunfire from these overnight amateurs.

She touched his arm tenderly. "You...saved me."

Jacob could smell the musky scent of her on her fingers. He grunted and began to walk across the glen, towards the trail through the trees.

"Wait," she called. But he did not wait. He would meet her again, soon.

◆◆◆

Had he not known better, he would have thought the old woman's house abandoned. The panes in the windows had long since broken and the chimney had started to crumble. Mice droppings dusted the floor and leaves drifted over the furnishings, all which had been scratched to shreds.

But live here, she had. Year in and year out, deep in the woods, far from the path, not easily found. But Jacob, who knew every foot of the forest, had always known of the cottage and been curious about its mysterious owner. He'd seen her often enough— creeping through the trees, howling at the moon, picking her teeth with a twig. But what did she eat, young Jacob wondered, for the old woman kept no garden or chicken coop and never went to town.

When he'd asked his mother what the old woman in the woods ate, she'd ruffled his hair and told him the house and all that was in it was made of gingerbread, and wouldn't that be wonderful? Jacob scoffed at such a tall-tale. The only gingerbread that interested Jacob was that baked by Emily's father. Every winter season, the bakery sold gingerbread cookies shaped like girls in stiff dresses and painted with chocolate hair, a rather pedestrian likeness of Emily, but Emily all the same.

And so Jacob never asked his mother about the old woman in the woods again, and had not thought of the her in over a decade. But when Emily and the baby were killed, Jacob knew he would have to return to the cottage for here, his gut said, he would discover the truth.

He'd waited out the month and come last night, when the moon was full. And under the revealing power of the moon, he'd done what he'd planned to execute. Now, he waited again. But as for a plan, he was unsure. He hoped that whatever actions he ought to take would become clear when she arrived.

Jacob installed himself in a dilapidated armchair to wait. His hand held a glass filled with amber liquid. Last night, he'd not drank all the whisky. He sipped in silence. Mice scampered in the dark corners. An owl landed on the windowsill, tracking the vermin with large golden eyes. A moment later it swooped inside the cottage, caught one up in its talons and was gone. And she—well, she would arrive soon enough.

The liquor had settled warmly into his bones when he heard footsteps on the porch. The door opened with a crack and Red entered the cottage, pushing back the hood from her face.

Jacob did not move, watching her from the shadows, the glass of whisky in his hand, half way to his mouth. But he knew that she saw him in the dark for her eyes widened with surprise and she dropped the picnic basket. Sausages rolled onto the floor.

"What are you doing in my grandmother's house?" she demanded. She made no move to pick up the basket of food. She lifted her hands to unfasten her red cloak. It fell to the floor, puddling around her feet like a pool of spilt blood.

"I came because the King decreed it," Jacob replied. But he did not come for the King. Only for Emily and the baby.

Moonlight beamed through the window and fell upon her, silvering her skin, hair and teeth. His eyes traced the lithe form of her body beneath her scarlet dress, as though she was once again naked at the riverside. His steadfast gaze landed at her breastbone, where her heart was safely stowed behind. He longed to place his hand over her heart, to feel its tempo, to understand its nature.

"Your eyes are always upon me," she observed, moving closer. Then she placed a hand over her heart, disrupting his view, and began to unbutton her bodice. She peeled away the garment, tossing it onto Jacob's lap, and rubbed her hands over her breasts, stiffening her pink nipples. "You like raspberries, I think?"

But for putting aside his drink, Jacob did not move. The threadbare armchair was not comfortable, but he had perched on many jagged rocks and spiny branches in his time. A sniper does not complain of his post.

Once divested of her bodice, she dropped her skirt and twirled her fingertips in the downy fur beneath her navel. His eyes tracked her hands as she moved them over her body. Then she kneeled at his feet and ran small white fingers over his leather-clad thighs. His own thick fingers dug into the armrests of the chair. "You look because you like to, Stalker?" she coaxed.

He could not lie. Jacob nodded, stilling her hands with his own. He pressed his thumbs into her palms and kneaded her hands, fighting violent urges to take her. "Yes. Yes, I like to look. You are beautiful, girl in red."

Red arched closer to him. "I take your breath away?" she groaned, brushing his lips with her own.

He closed his eyes and she kissed him. He exhaled. Yes, she tugged on his breath and unraveled it from his throat. He groaned softly to himself as he thought of Emily and her song.

His eyes flew open. Emily was not there. Only the old woman's granddaughter.

He looked at her breasts, firm as apples, hanging only inches from his mouth as she clambered onto his lap. He thought of Emily. Her pulse beat in her delicate neck. He thought of Emily. The moon shadowed the weakest point of her mandible.

He found his voice, wound tight with need: "Your grandmother—"

"—is not home," she crooned.

"—is in the other room," he finished.

Red cocked an eyebrow. "In the bedroom?" she whispered. Gooseflesh rose on her skin.

Jacob nodded. "In the bedroom."

She climbed off of him and stood to take his hand, leading him across the cottage parlour to a closed door. He wanted to dig his fingers into her bare bottom, white as a doe's, and open her legs wide. But he stayed his course, following her lead.

She put her other hand on the doorknob and turned. Jacob released her hand as she entered the bedroom, and quietly lifted his rifle from its holster.

She neither screamed or wept. She uttered not a word. She only drew up to the side of the bed and laid a gentle hand on the dead werewolf's chest. A single silver bullet lodged deep inside, its entry point blackened with dry blood. She shuddered and turned to him at last. "You did this?"

"Last night, when the moon was full," he confessed. He watched her carefully, gauging her reaction. Wondering.

"For a bounty!" she spat, suddenly enraged, and she rushed at him, teeth bared. He pushed her away and she tumbled onto the bed, her bare limbs tangling among the shaggy grey ones of her grandmother.

"Not for a bounty," he shouted, looming over the naked girl, for he had no intention of claiming the King's prize. He'd killed the old werewolf for revenge, not for reward. And in that moment, he had understood his grandfather's lust for the kill.

Red put her arm around his neck and pulled him closer. "You have ended her misery, Hunter, for she detested her life." Her breath on his skin was hot and sticky. "And for that, I'm indebted."

Jacob could feel the warmth of her body pressed against his, and he sunk onto the bed, dropping his rifle to the floor. The mattress groaned under their weight. The body of the werewolf was cold and stunk of rotten meat. He shoved it hard and it toppled off the bed.

The girl spread her legs and wrapped them around Jacob's torso. "I brought her food every week, that she might not have to eat the vermin of the woods." Red's lips curled back over her teeth and she snarled. "Imagine her torture—a lifetime of eating rats when all she ever craved was the meat of one little baby!" Her pink tongue darted out of her mouth and dragged itself along his neck. "What kind of torture grips you, Hunter?"

"You," he replied, for she scattered his senses.

"Stupid hound dog!" She laughed and nipped the flesh of his throat. "I am not your torture, Hunter, I am your delight! For you would lick me dry in a heartbeat. No, I will not torture you," she hissed, "for I wish to save you. As you saved me."

But he had not saved her in the clearing. No, he had only fought the other bounty hunter because he had wanted her for himself. All of her—her cool, dry skin. Her warm, moist openings. Her softly beating heart.

She responded to his mounting desire by moving rhythmically against him. "What a sorry life you lead, Hunter—heartbroken and hungry. Hungry as a wolf. You want to learn everything about me, but you will not see it on the surface." She bayed at the moon and bucked her hips against his. "Tell me,

Hunter, will you take me?"

And Jacob wondered. Without Emily, what happiness there was to be found in his life? Could it be found here, thrust inside Red? He buried his face in her hair and inhaled. It smelled like the river. The trees. The woods. She smelled not unlike her grandmother had, the nights he had surveilled the cottage.

Red moved against him, luring him into the folds of her limbs. The hairs on his neck tingled. With pleasure? The blood pounding through his veins made it difficult to sense his own certainty. Could danger be confused for desire? He thought of Emily again. He reminded himself that the greatest happiness without her was to avenge her death.

Red writhed beneath him, calling him back. "You may take me, dog, anyway you like."

He lifted his face from the nest of her hair and placed a finger between her breasts, where he lightly traced a line along her sternum. He said nothing, struggling for a glimpse of the truth, as a rabbit in a snare struggles to be free.

"Here?" she pursued, using her hands to push her breasts against either side of his finger. Her eyes flashed in the darkness, seeking his. "You would put it here?"

Jacob closed his eyes for a moment, desperate to know all that she claimed was hidden beneath the surface of her body. He sighed and dropped his other arm over the side of the bed, searching for his rifle. His hand found the weapon and lifted it. His finger sought out the trigger. He looked in her eyes, questioning. Demanding she somehow show him the answer.

Jacob lifted the gun and placed the barrel against her breastbone. He spoke. "Yes. Should it be true, I would put it here…"

# K.M. Tremills

K.M. Tremills is the creative author of the *Great Lands* series. Kate began her career writing for the film industry and received support from the Canadian Film Centre, National Screen Institute, and Telefilm Canada. She contributed articles to Elle Canada and Moving Pictures and screened a film at the Cannes and Toronto Film Festivals. Kate was lured back to her first love — novels — when *Messenger* appeared and demanded to be written. She is currently writing her second novel, *Blue Moon*, and contributing to *Fabled*, a collection of short stories with Kathryn and Roberta Cottam. She also travels for pleasure and inspiration, gathering stories from Ireland to New York City. Kate is always delighted to hear from readers at **www.kmtremills.com.**

Roaming the world for inspiration makes Kate as joyful as a robin in springtime.

# Kathryn Cottam

Kathryn Cottam holds a B.A. in English Literature from the University of Victoria and is a graduate of the Vancouver Film School Screenwriting Program. Kathryn has been both a story editor and screenwriting judge. Her script, *Bus Station Zombies*, was a semi-finalist at the Austin Film Festival Writing Competition and her first novel, *The Shoemaker: A Tale of Love, Magic & Unnatural Acts* was published last year by Fox Tale Press and was nominated for best Fantasy Novel of 2013 by *InD'Tale Magazine*. Visit her website at **www.kathrycottam.com**

A gothic novel, a cup of tea and a blustery storm is Kathryn's idea of a perfect evening.

# Roberta Cottam

Roberta's short fiction and poetry is published in several issues of *The Claremont Review* and been featured in the anthology, *Naming the Baby*. *Shakespearian Shopping Theatre*, co-written with her sister Kathryn Cottam, was short-listed for The Arts Club in Vancouver. She holds a BFA with distinction from the University of Victoria and was a faculty member of the Art Institute of Vancouver where she taught one of her favourite subjects, Costume History. Roberta has illustrated for several international brands, including Lululemon, and has collaborated on clothing designs with Nelly Furtado and Joe Jonas through the non-profit organization, Me to We. Find her online at **www.robertacottam.com**

Roberta believes a woman's most beautiful quality is her sense of adventure.

*Also by K. M. Tremills*

# Messenger

Torn from her family and sent into exile, Gabriella thinks of only one thing: retribution. The Great Prince ripped her Kingdom apart when he declared war on her parents and imprisoned her sister, Hannah, in his palace. Now the true rulers are in hiding and Gabriella is on the run.

Despite a promise to stay safe, Gabriella sets out across the Great Lands to save Hannah. On the way, she meets Adrian, a mysterious guide, and discovers that her journey involves greater peril than an urgent rescue mission. Gabriella risks the Great Prince discovering her deepest secret. And if he does, all hope for her world will be lost forever.

*Arriving Fall 2014 by K. M. Tremills*

# BLUE MOON

BOOK ONE IN THE FATED SERIES

Welcome to Manhattan's Upper East Side. A place occupied by the sisters of Fate, three women who have maintained order for millennia by orchestrating every mortal life. Until a dark force rises out of the shadows; resentful of their power and determined to challenge immortal control.

Into their world, comes free-spirited Helen Troy. Helen dances her way through life. Inventing the moves as she goes and assuming she is in charge. Then she meets Fitzgerald Logon, long-time associate of the Fates. And Helen suddenly discovers her choices are not always her own.

Logon and the Fates recognize Helen's gift. Her spontaneity works counter to their structured immortal ways and is exactly what they need to take on their adversary. With her on their side, the Fates might prevent humanity from reverting to a dark age of unbridled violence.

But can they convince Helen, who has always put herself first, to risk her life for the sake of the gods? And is she ready to confront the most unpredictable force the Fates have ever faced?

ravenheart

*Also by Kathryn Cottam*

# SHOEMAKER
*A Tale of Love, Magic & Unnatural Acts*

Lowly shoemaker Edward Cordwainer is desperate for a better life, and so he enters an arranged marriage with Anastasia, a wealthy merchant's daughter with scars of her own. But when the wedding doesn't lead to luxury and love, Edward succumbs to an erotic encounter with a mysterious woman, resulting in a magical bargain to become the most famous man in all the kingdom.

As the magic takes root, Edward becomes wealthy and well-known, not to mention the latest plaything of the Princess Ambrosia, who gets anything—and anyone—she desires.

But magic is a cruel lover. As Edward's star rises, darkness envelops Houndstooth when the women of the town start to disappear.

As events unfold, Edward's one simple wish threatens to destroy his world…

Fox Tale
PRESS

*Also by Roberta Cottam and Kathryn Cottam*

# BLUEBEARD'S
# BRIDE

When sisters Margaret and Rosie Jaye receive word of their sister Helen's death, they journey to the isolated Blueford Manor. Seemingly cast in an eternal twilight, the estate proves to be full of mysteries: their niece's inexplicable illness, housemaids who never stay longer than a season and a thriving bat colony.

As Rosie and Margaret unravel the web of lies surrounding Helen's death, the sisters become entangled in life at Blueford Manor. So much so, that Rosie decides to stay—forever.

Unsettled by Rosie's decision, Margaret suspects Helen's widower, the formidable Captain Ford, of influencing her sister. But Margaret's quest for answers is thwarted when Rosie suddenly disappears within the walls of Blueford Manor.

As Margaret sets out to unlock the truth, she makes another startling discovery. Adept with a needle and thread, Margaret possesses a dark and unnatural power of her own. Now, Margaret must solve her sister's disappearance and the unanswered questions of Helen's death before Rosie, too, is counted among the dead.

Fox Tale
PRESS

*Arriving Fall 2014 by K. M. Tremills,*
*Kathryn Cottam & Roberta Cottam*

# FABLED

## 17 TALES YOU THINK YOU KNOW

*Twelve Dancing Princesses*
*Rumplestilskin*
*Pandora's Box*
*& other stories you thought you knew*

A volume of seventeen contemporary stories inspired by fairy tales, myths and nursery rhymes.

From the bestselling authors of *Messenger*, *The Shoemaker: A Tale of Love, Magic & Unnatural Acts* and *Bluebeard's Bride*.

Fox Tale
PRESS